STAR WARS™

BEYOND THE WORLD OF COLOURING

EGMONT
We bring stories to life

Star Wars Art Therapy Colouring Book first published in Great Britain 2016
by Egmont UK Limited © & ™ 2016 Lucasfilm Ltd.

Dot-to-Dot Star Wars first published in Great Britain 2016 by Egmont UK Limited
© & ™ 2016 Lucasfilm Ltd.

Star Wars Galaxy of Colouring first published in Great Britain 2016 by Egmont UK Limited
© & ™ 2016 Lucasfilm Ltd.

Star Wars Colouring by Numbers first published in Great Britain 2016 by Egmont UK Limited
© & ™ 2016 Lucasfilm Ltd.

This edition published in Great Britain 2016
by Egmont UK Limited, The Yellow Building,
1 Nicholas Road, London W11 4AN
© & ™ 2016 Lucasfilm Ltd.

ISBN 978 0 6035 7298 2
66833/1
Printed in Poland

For more great *Star Wars* books, visit www.egmont.co.uk/starwars

No part of this publication may be reproduced, stored in a retrieval system, or transmitted in any form
or by any means, electronic, mechanical, photocopying or otherwise, without the prior consent of the copyright owner.

Stay safe online. Any website addresses listed in this book are correct at the time of going to print. However, Egmont is
not responsible for content hosted by third parties. Please be aware that online content can be subject to change and websites
can contain content that is unsuitable for children. We advise that all children are supervised when using the internet.

ANTI-STRESS
COLOURING

STAR WARS™

INTRODUCTION

Relax, turn the page, and to paraphrase Yoda:

"May the colouring force be with you."

Immerse yourself in a galaxy far, far away by colouring this
collection of drawings and original works from the movies you love.
Enjoy this artistic and mindful activity whilst creating stunning
images of your favourite ships, droids and characters.

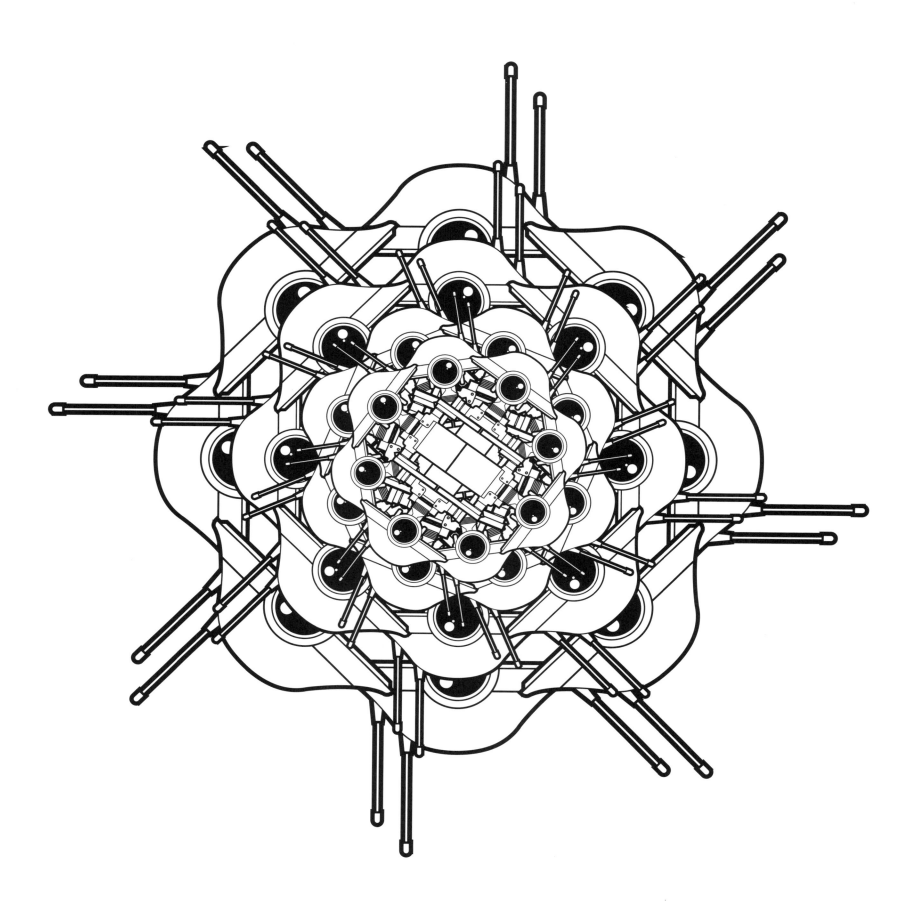

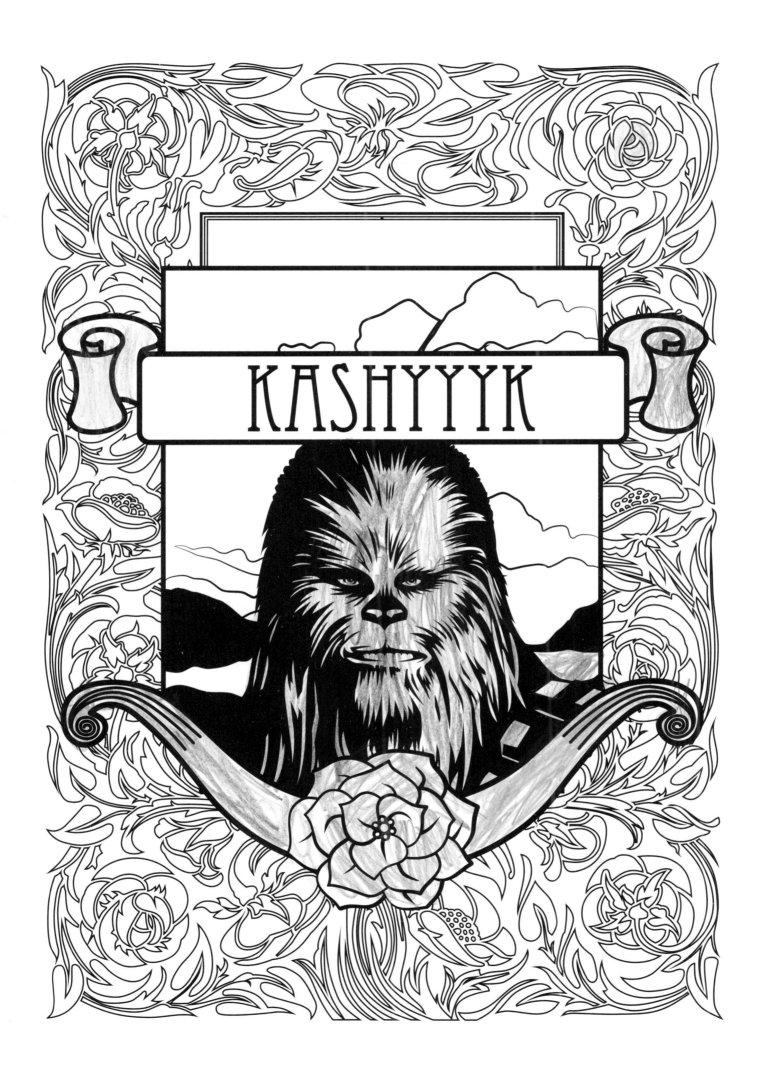

KASHYYYK

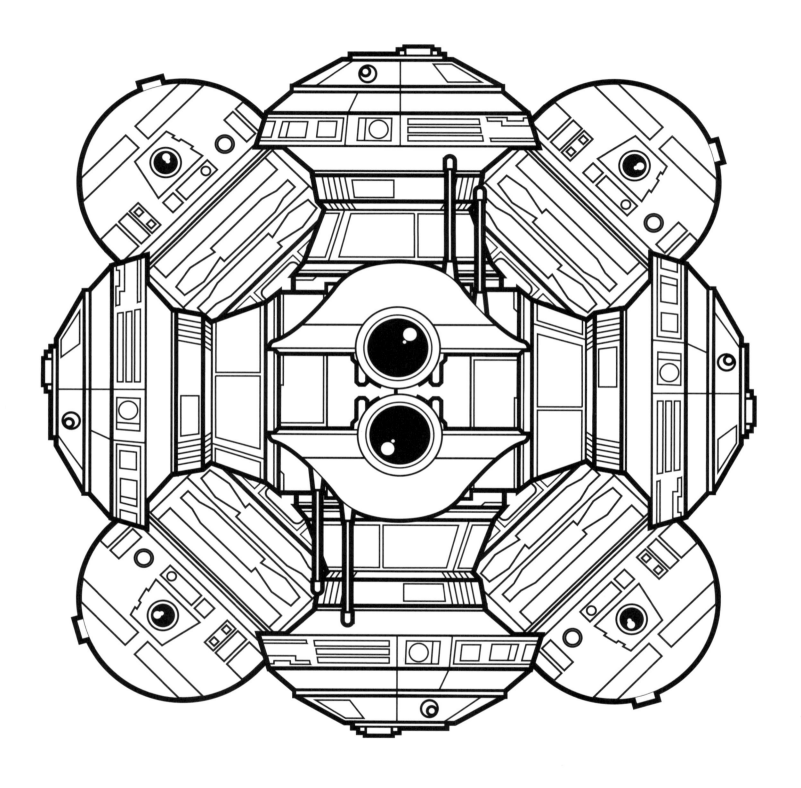

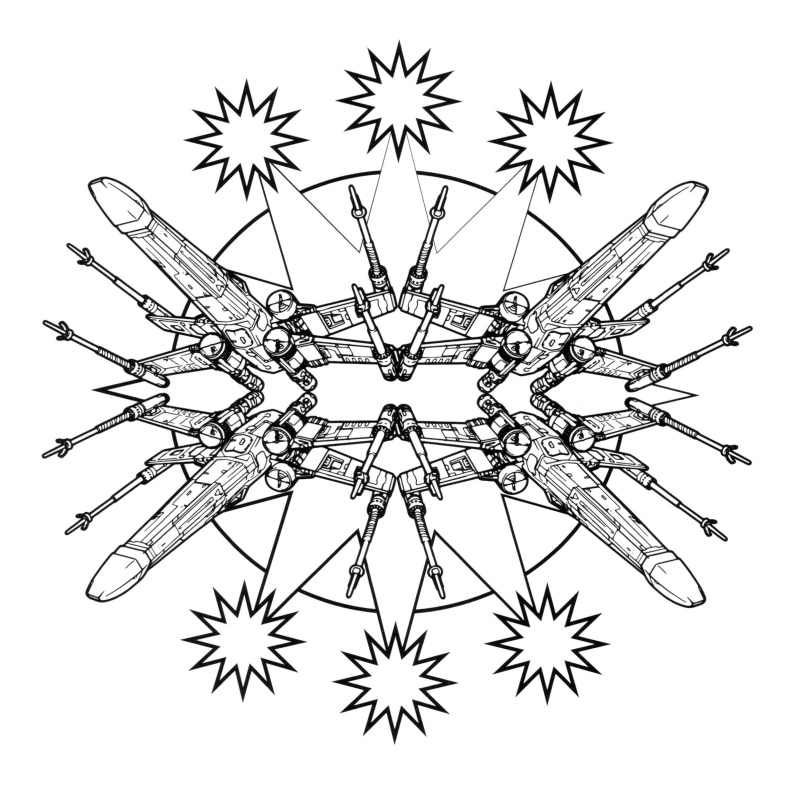

DOT-TO-DOT

STAR WARS™

Illustrations by Jérémy Mariez

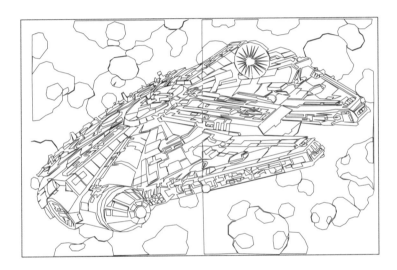

INTRODUCTION

In the following pages watch as rebel ships, leaders of the Resistance, vessels of the Empire, droids and Jedi Masters unfold before you. Find the number 1 and follow the path from point to point to reveal characters, ships and aliens that inhabit the *Star Wars* universe.

Some illustrations are composed of several pieces: follow the same colour points before moving on to the next colour. The number with the circle around it is where you begin, and the number with the box around it is the end of that sequence of numbers. Then, if you like, you can colour in your creations.

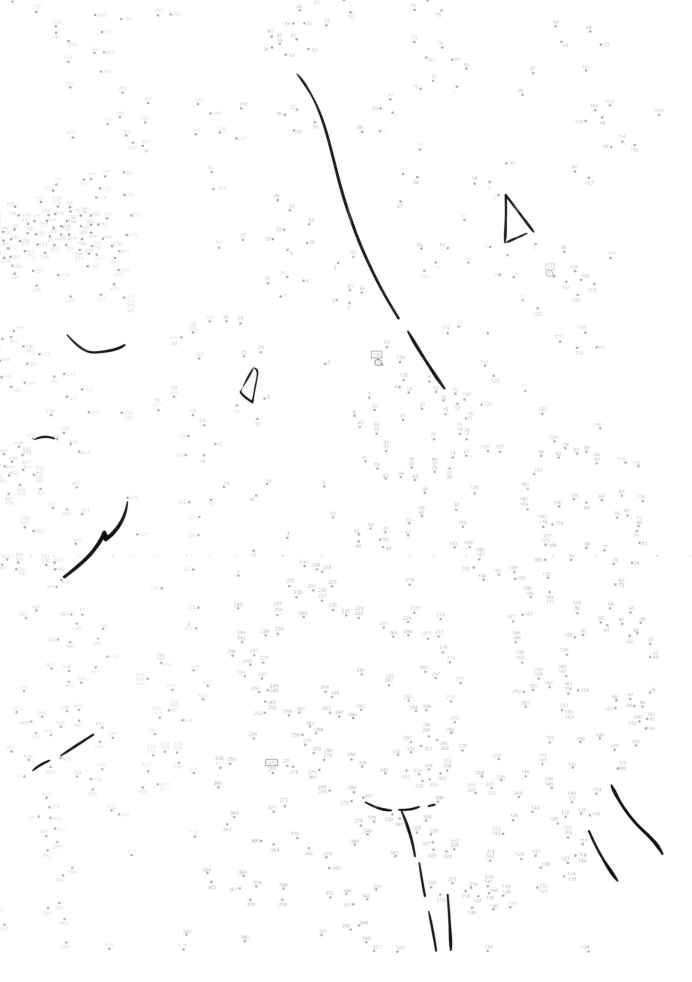

90

SOLUTIONS

50

C-3PO and R2-D2 go to Jabba's Palace

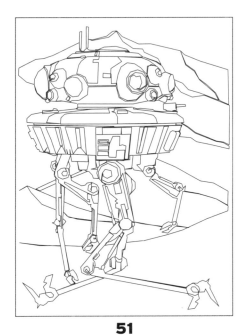

51

Probe droid is sent to Hoth to detect rebel presence

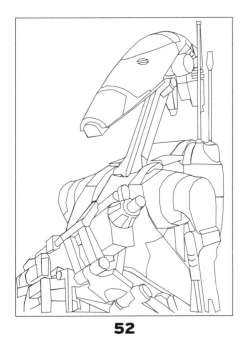

52

B1 battle droid of the Trade Federation

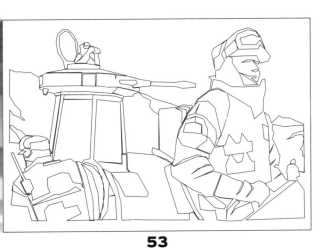

53

The rebels on Hoth

54

Luke and his tauntaun on Hoth

55

Chancellor Palpatine of the Galactic Senate

56

*Count Dooku, leader of the
Separatist Alliance*

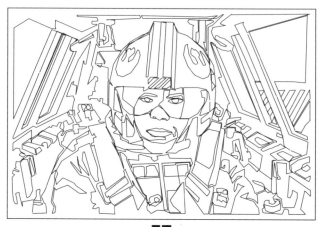

57

A rebel pilot

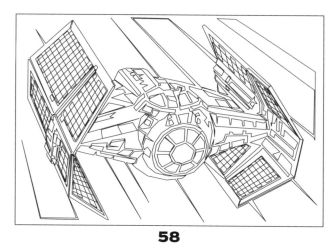

58

Darth Vader's TIE fighter

59

Han Solo in carbonite

60 & 61

The Emperor

62

*Boba Fett, the Mandalorian
bounty hunter*

63

Lando Calrissian, Baron Administrator of Cloud City

64

View of Cloud City

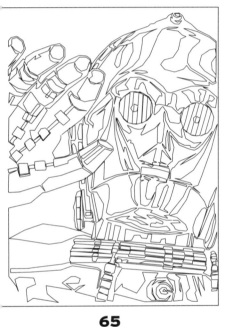

65

C-3PO, protocol droid

66

R2-D2, astromech droid

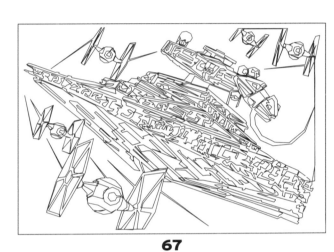

67

Imperial-class Star Destroyer

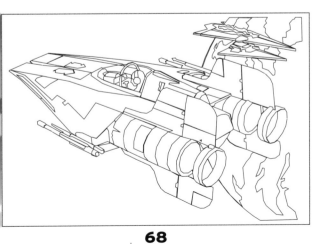

68

A-wing, a Rebel Alliance starfighter

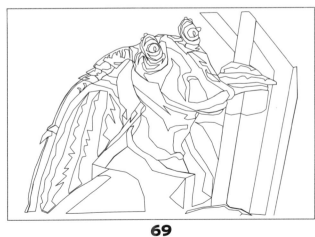

69

Jar Jar Binks, Gungan living on Naboo

70

Leia Organa

71

Jedi Master Obi-Wan Kenobi

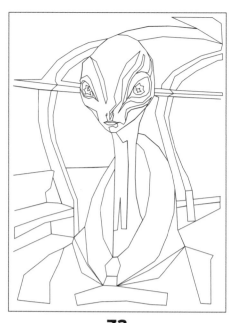

72

A Kaminoan

73

Anakin Skywalker before the Jedi Council

74

Yoda, Grand Master of the Jedi Order

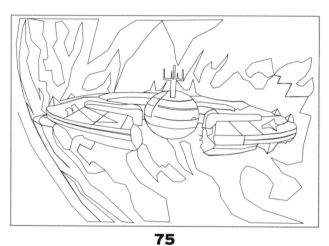

75

Trade Federation ship

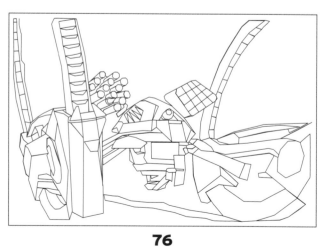

76

Tank class Hailfire droid IG-227

77

Wicket W Warwick, an Ewok

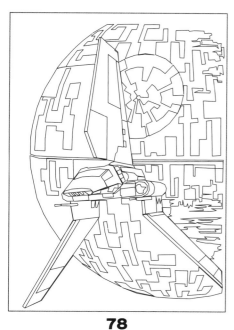

78

Tydirium, *Imperial shuttle stolen by the rebels to destroy the second Death Star*

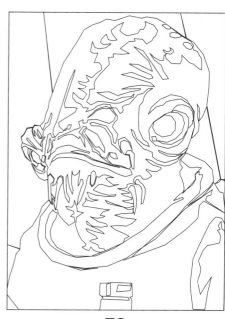

79

Admiral Ackbar, who coordinates the rebel attack in Return of the Jedi

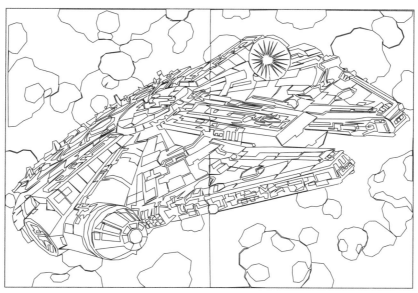

80 & 81

The Millennium Falcon

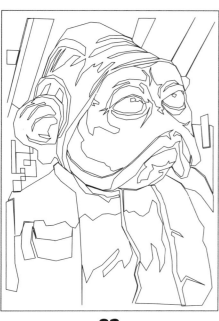

82

Nien Nunb, co-pilot to Lando Calrissian on board the Millennium Falcon during the battle of Endor

83

Anakin Skywalker/Darth Vader

84

Dexter Jettster, owner of Dex's Diner on Coruscant

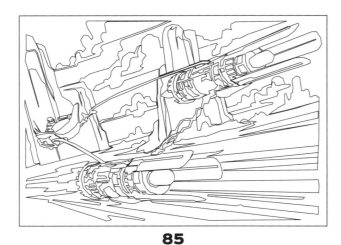

85

Boonta Eve Classic - podrace on Tatooine

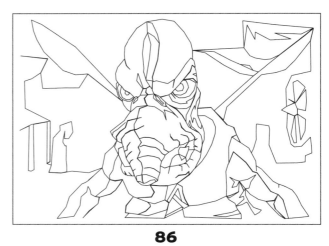

86

Watto, Toydarian living on Tatooine, owner of young Anakin Skywalker and his mother, Shmi

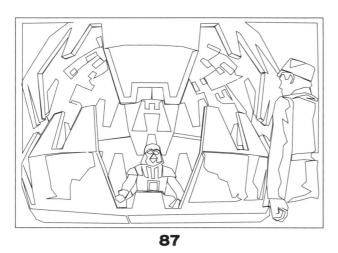

87

Darth Vader's meditation chamber

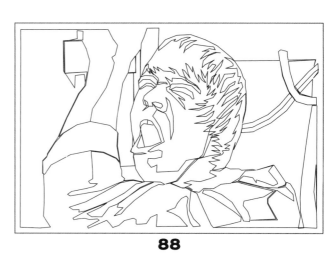

88

Luke Skywalker learns the truth about his father

89

Luke Skywalker

90

Old Ben Kenobi

GALAXY OF
COLOURING

STAR
WARS
™

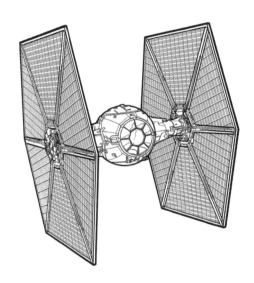

INTRODUCTION

We all have our favourite memories of the *Star Wars* saga:
a character that has made a deep impression on us,
a scene, a line, a touching moment ...

Immerse yourself in a galaxy far, far away by colouring this
collection of drawings and original works from the movies you love.
Enjoy this artistic and mindful activity whilst creating stunning
images of your favourite ships, droids and characters.

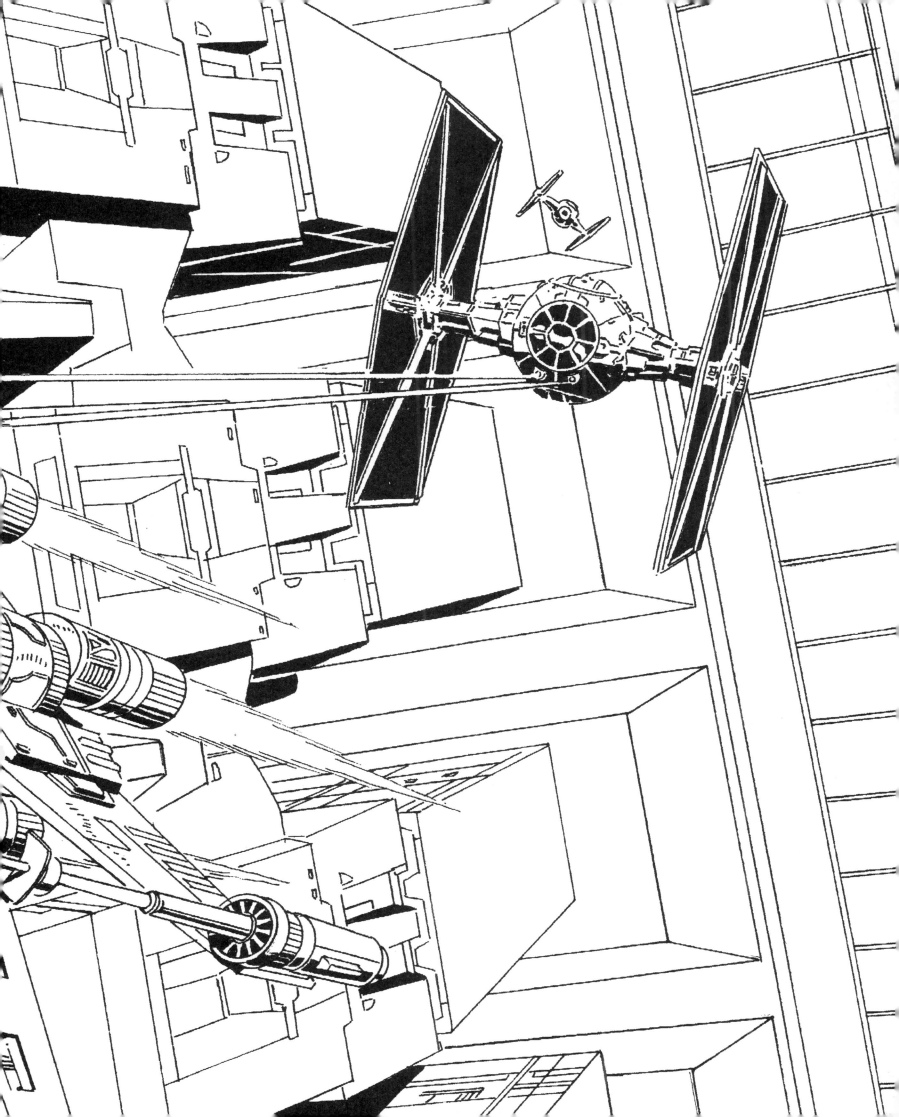

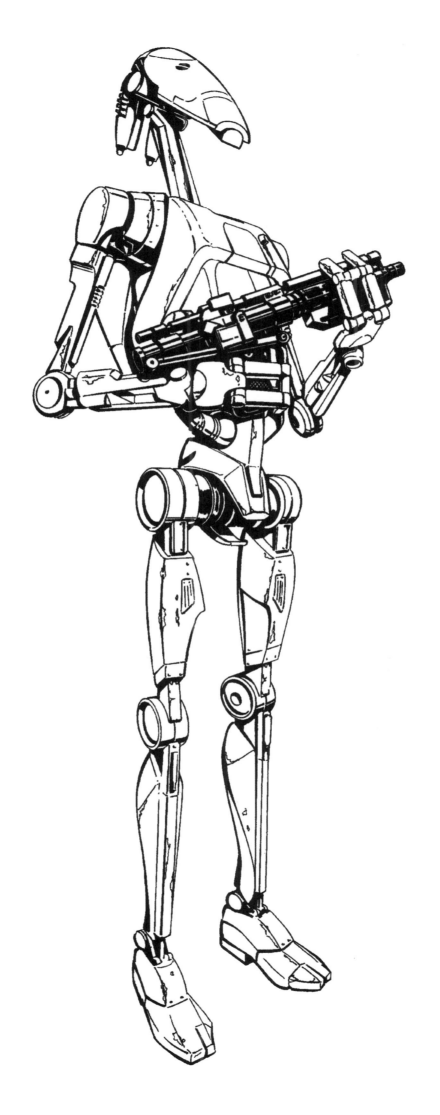

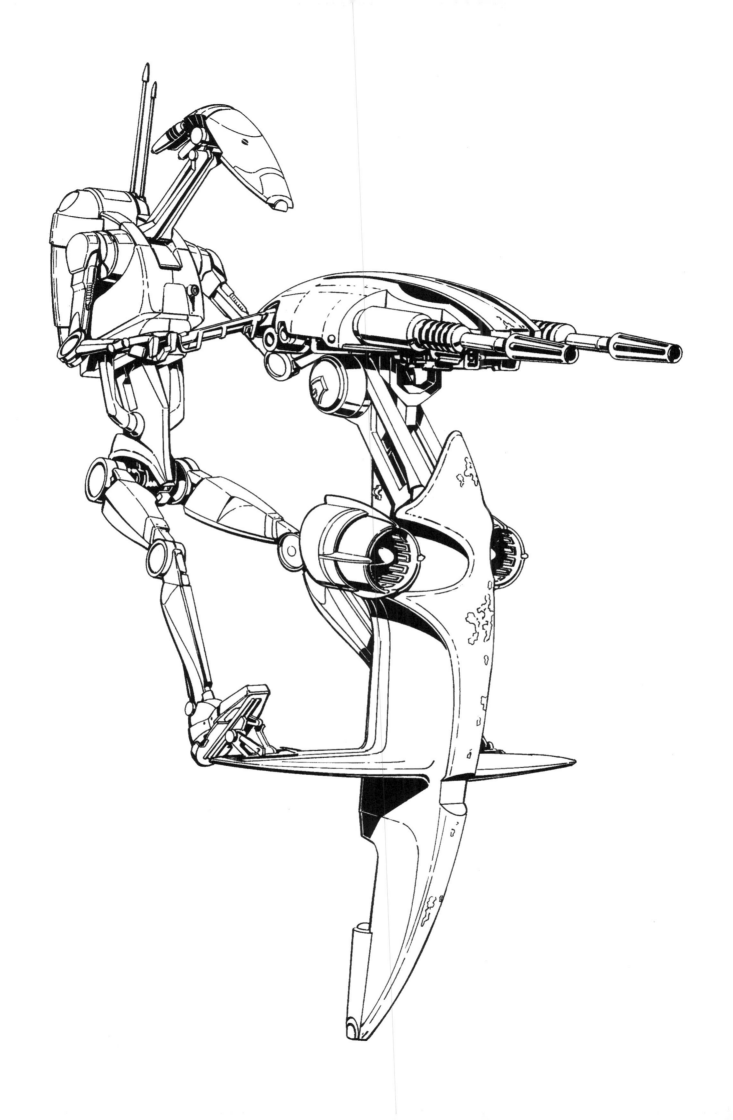

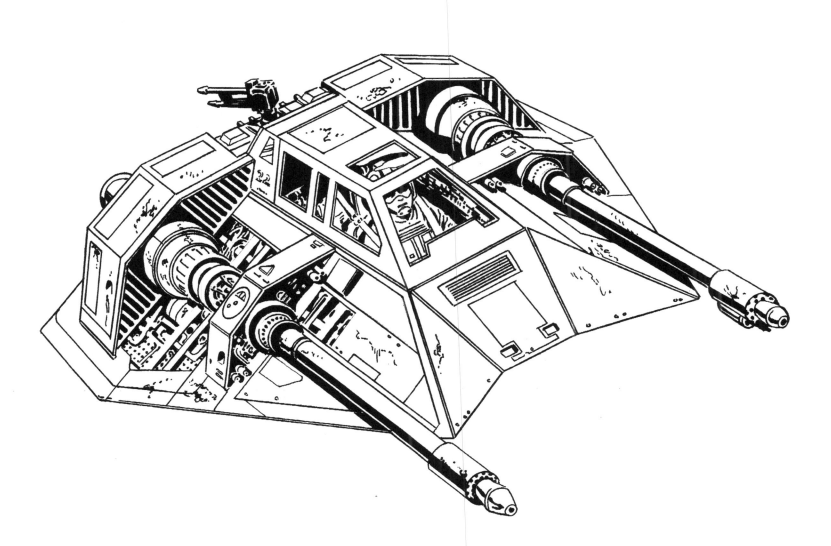

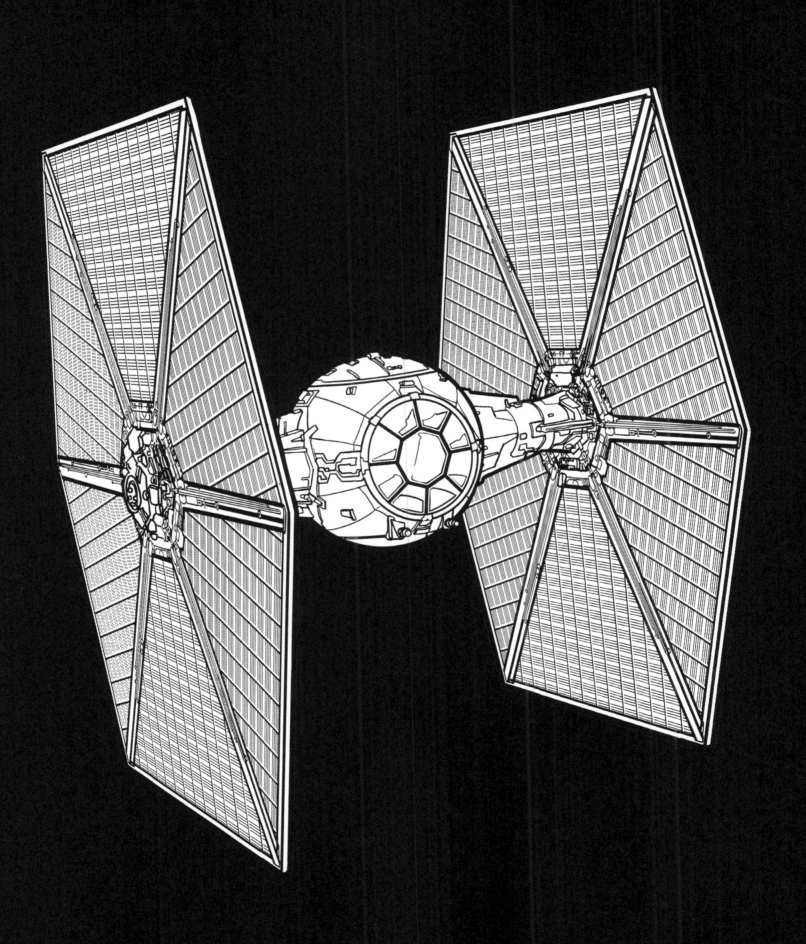

143

COLOURING
BY NUMBERS

STAR WARS
™

INTRODUCTION

Explore over 40 mysteries through colour that will help you to relax and rediscover the movies you love. Using the colour codes, unravel the intertwining lines, apply each shade to the corresponding zone and bring to life the characters, vessels and droids of *Star Wars*.

As you colour, will you find Darth Vader or the Emperor? Obi-Wan Kenobi or Anakin Skywalker? Queen Amidala or Princess Leia? Each new colour reveals a little more of the final picture.

1 2 3 4 5 6 7 8 9

1 2 3 4 5 6 7 8 9 0 A B C

1 2 3 4 5 6 7 8 9 0 A B C

1 2 3 4 5 6 7

1 **2** **3** **4** **5** **6** **7** **8** **9** **0** **A** **B** **C** **D** **E**

1 2 3 4 5 6 7 8 9 0 A B C

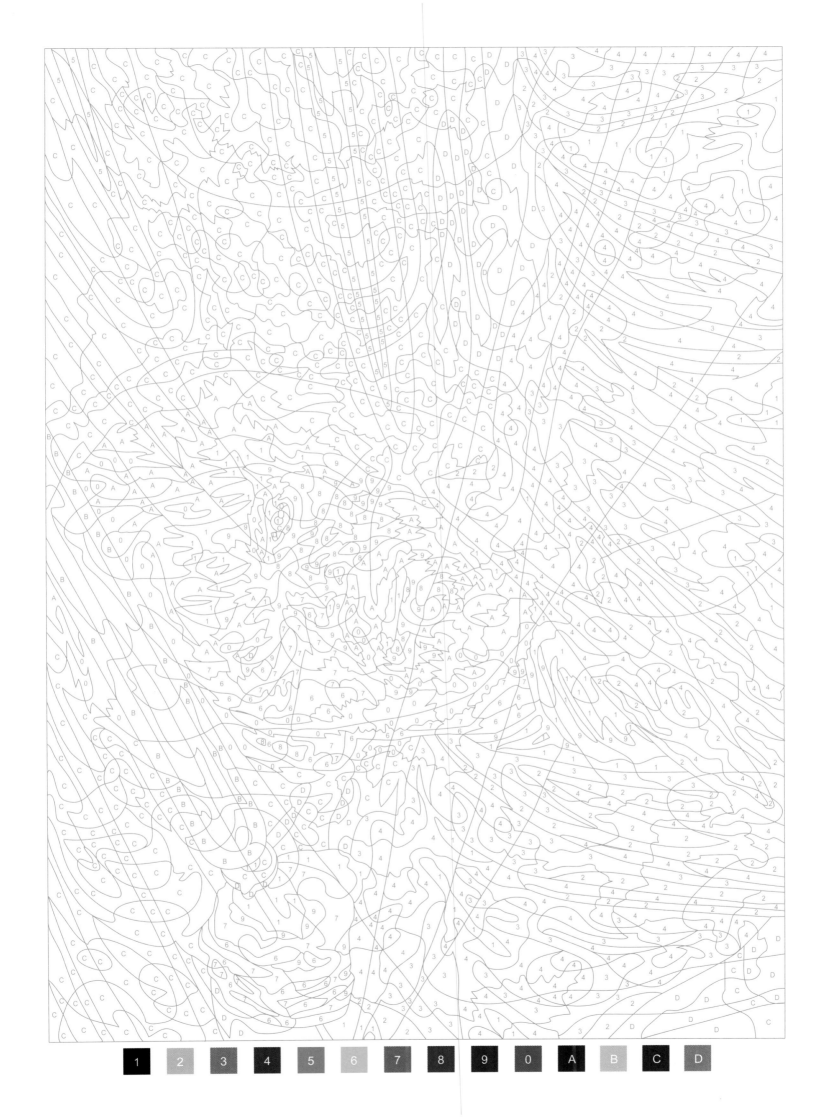

1 2 3 4 5 6 7 8 9 0 A B C

159

1 2 3 4 5 6 7 8 9 0 A B

161

1 **2** **3** **4** **5** **6** **7** **8** **9** **0** **A** **B** **C** **D** **E**

1 2 3 4 5 6 7 8 9 0 A B C

171

175

1 2 3 4 5 6 7 8 9 0 A B C D

1 2 3 4 5 6 7 8 9

177

1 2 3 4 5 6 7 8 9 0 A B C D E

1 2 3 4 5 6 7 8 9 0 A B C D E

183

SOLUTIONS

146
DARTH VADER

147
DARTH MAUL

148
PADMÉ AMIDALA

149
LEIA ORGANA

150
C-3PO

151
COUNT DOOKU

152
YODA

153
QUEEN AMIDALA

154
BOBA FETT

155
OBI-WAN KENOBI

156
KI-ADI-MUNDI

157
WICKET, EWOK FROM THE FOREST MOON OF ENDOR

158
JAR JAR BINKS

159
**DARTH VADER
ON HIS FUNERAL PYRE**

160
MACE WINDU

161
**BOUSHH. IN FACT, LEIA DISGUISED
AS BOUSHH TO INFILTRATE
JABBA'S PALACE**

162
ANAKIN SKYWALKER

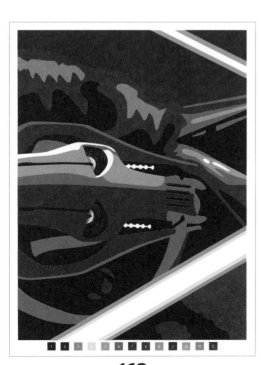

163
GENERAL GRIEVOUS

164
**EXTERIOR OF JABBA'S
PALACE ON TATOOINE**

165
LUKE SKYWALKER

166
ANAKIN SKYWALKER

167
QUI-GON JINN

168
BEN KENOBI

169
THE EMPEROR

170
A STORMTROOPER

171
HAN SOLO FROZEN IN CARBONITE

172
AT-ST

173
**ANAKIN SKYWALKER AFTER
HIS FALL TO THE DARK SIDE**

174
**ROYAL STARSHIP OF
THE QUEEN OF NABOO**

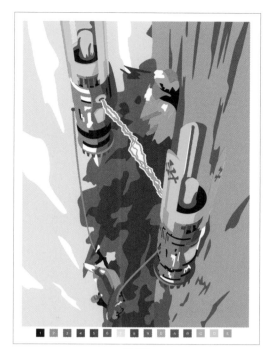

175
**ANAKIN SKYWALKER'S
PODRACER ON TATOOINE**

176
NIEN NUNB

177
JANGO FETT

178
YODA

179
THE EMPEROR

180
KIT FISTO

181
TUSKEN RAIDER

182
JABBA THE HUTT

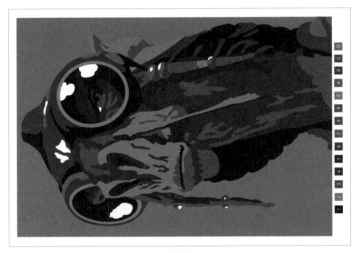

183
SEBULBA

184
CAPTAIN PHASMA

185
X-WING

186
REBEL PILOT